My FIRST Graphic Novel

RAH-RAH RUBY!

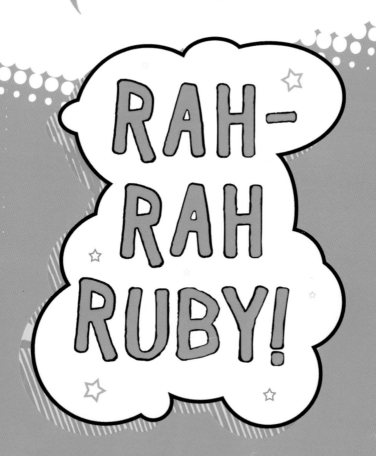

My First Graphic Novels are published by Stone Arch Books
151 Good Counsel Drive, P.O. Box 669
Mankato, Minnesota 56002
www.stonearchbooks.com

Library of Congress Cataloging-in-Publication Data
Jones, Christianne C.
    Rah-rah Ruby! / by Christianne C. Jones ; illustrated by Cori Doerrfeld.
    p. cm. — (My first graphic novel)
    ISBN 978-1-4342-1298-6 (library binding)
    ISBN 978-1-4342-1412-6 (pbk.)
    1. Graphic novels. [1. Graphic novels. 2. Cheerleading—Fiction.
3. English language—Spelling—Fiction.] I. Doerrfeld, Cori, ill. II. Title.
PZ7.7.J66Rah 2009
741.5'973—dc22   2008031972

Summary: Ruby loves cheerleading. She loves jumping, yelling, and flipping.
But when it's time to spell, Ruby freezes. Find out if Ruby learns to
spell in time to make the cheerleading squad.

Art Director: Heather Kindseth
Graphic Designer: Hilary Wacholz

1 2 3 4 5 6 14 13 12 11 10 09

Printed in the United States of America

My **FIRST** Graphic Novel

RAH-RAH RUBY!

by Christianne C. Jones
illustrated by Cori Doerrfeld

STONE ARCH BOOKS
www.stonearchbooks.com

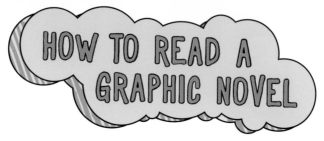

HOW TO READ A GRAPHIC NOVEL

Graphic novels are easy to read. Boxes called panels show you how to follow the story. Look at the panels from left to right and top to bottom.

Read the word boxes and word balloons from left to right as well. Don't forget the sound and action words in the pictures.

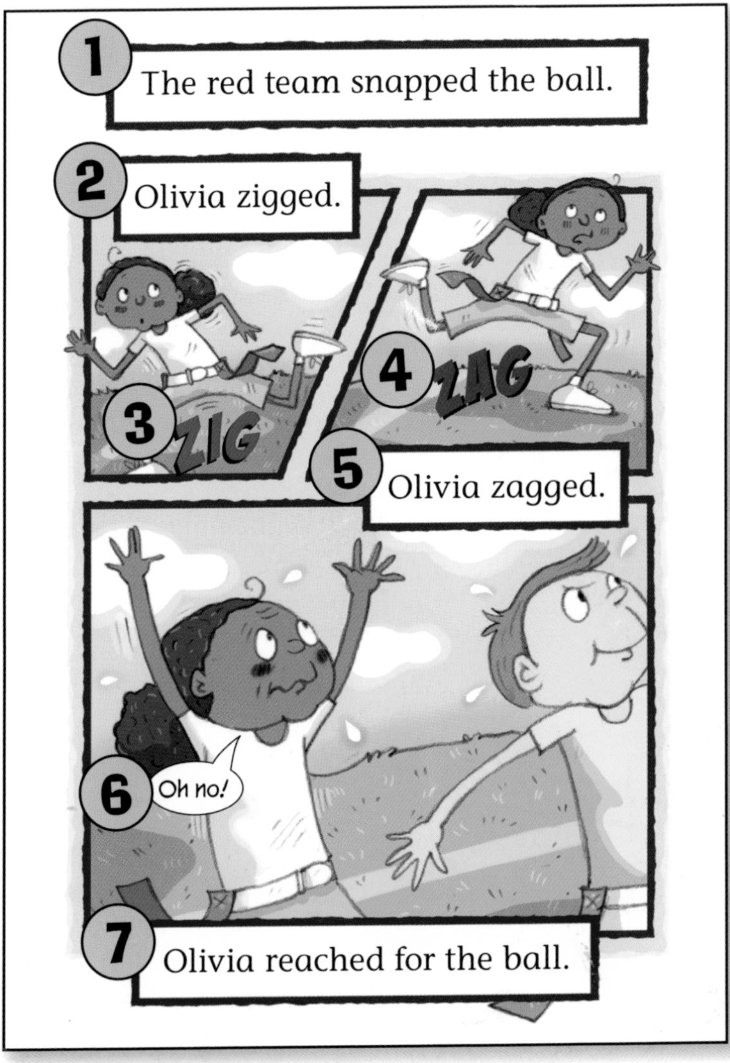
1
The red team snapped the ball.
2
Olivia zigged.
3
ZIG
4
ZAG
5
Olivia zagged.
6
Oh no!
7
Olivia reached for the ball.

The pictures and the words work together to tell the whole story.

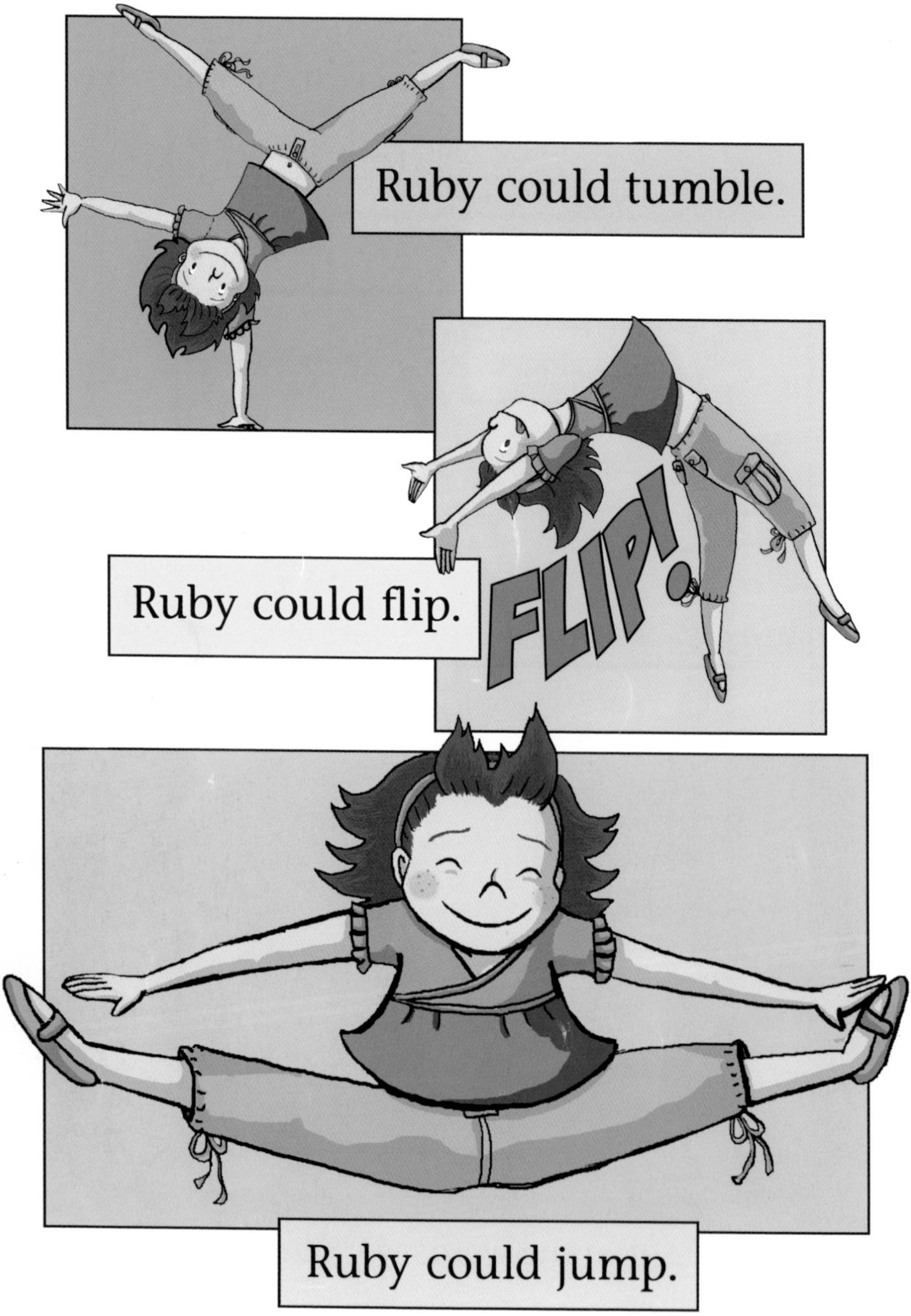
Ruby could tumble.
FLIP!
Ruby could flip.
Ruby could jump.

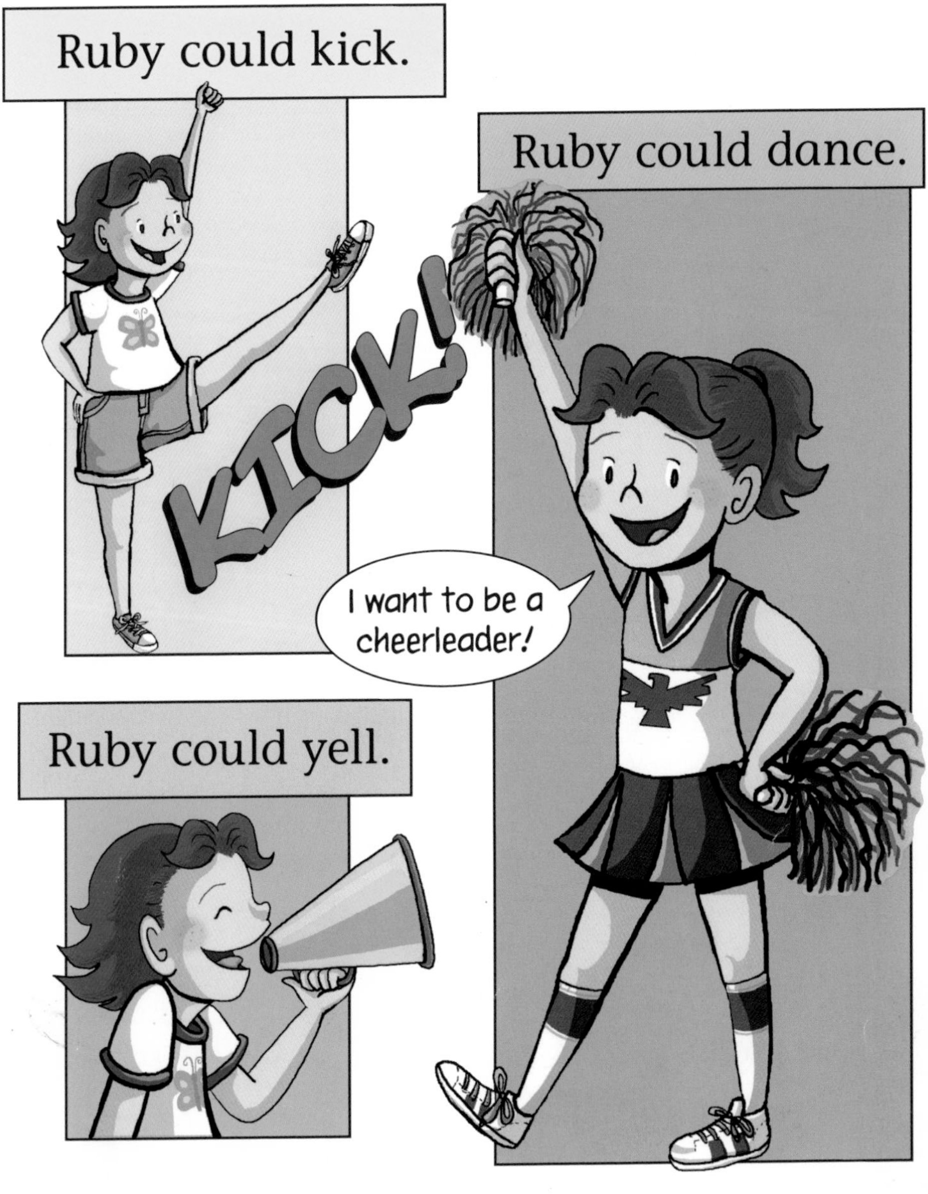
Ruby could kick.
KICK!
Ruby could dance.
I want to be a cheerleader!
Ruby could yell.

Ruby could shout the cheers.

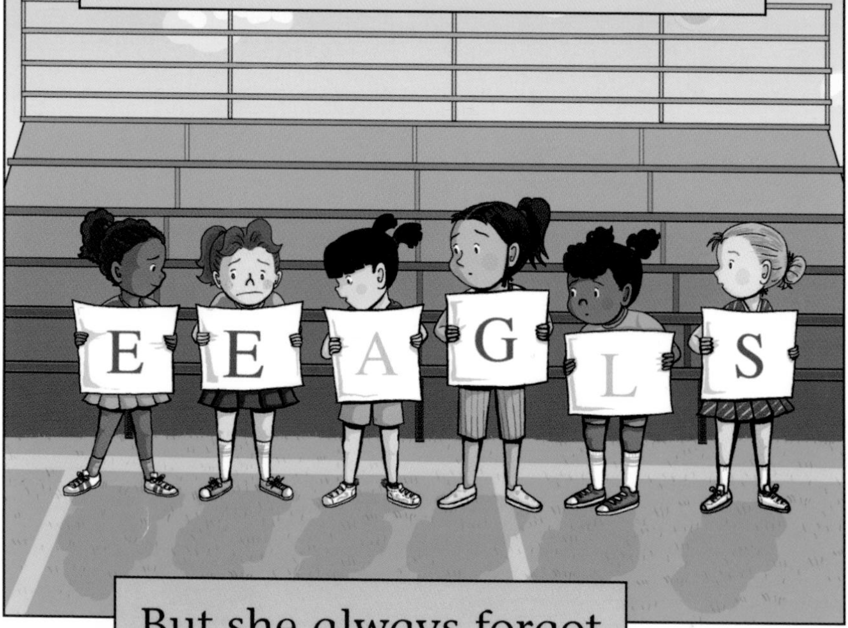
E
E
A
G
L
S

But she always forgot the spelling parts.

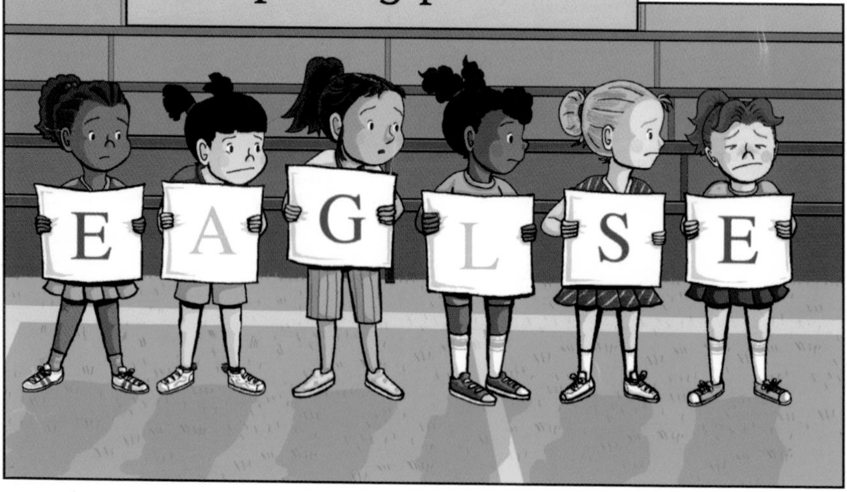
E
A
G
L
S
E

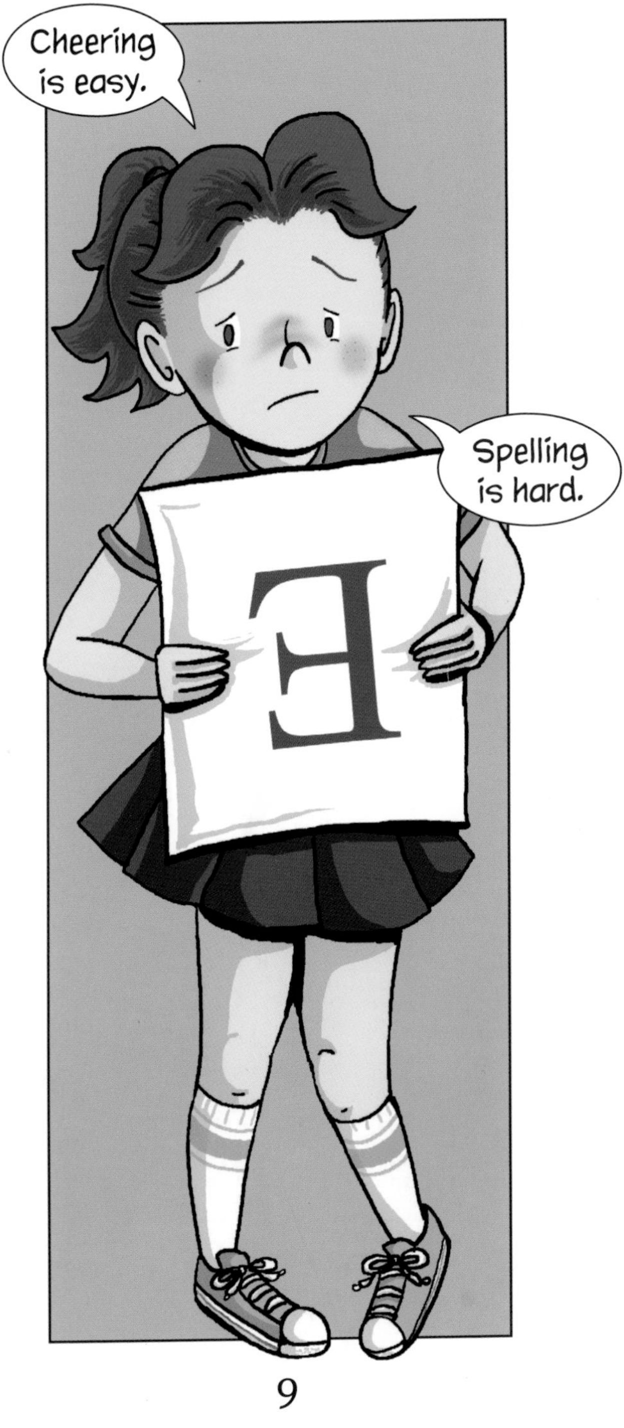
Cheering is easy.
Spelling is hard.

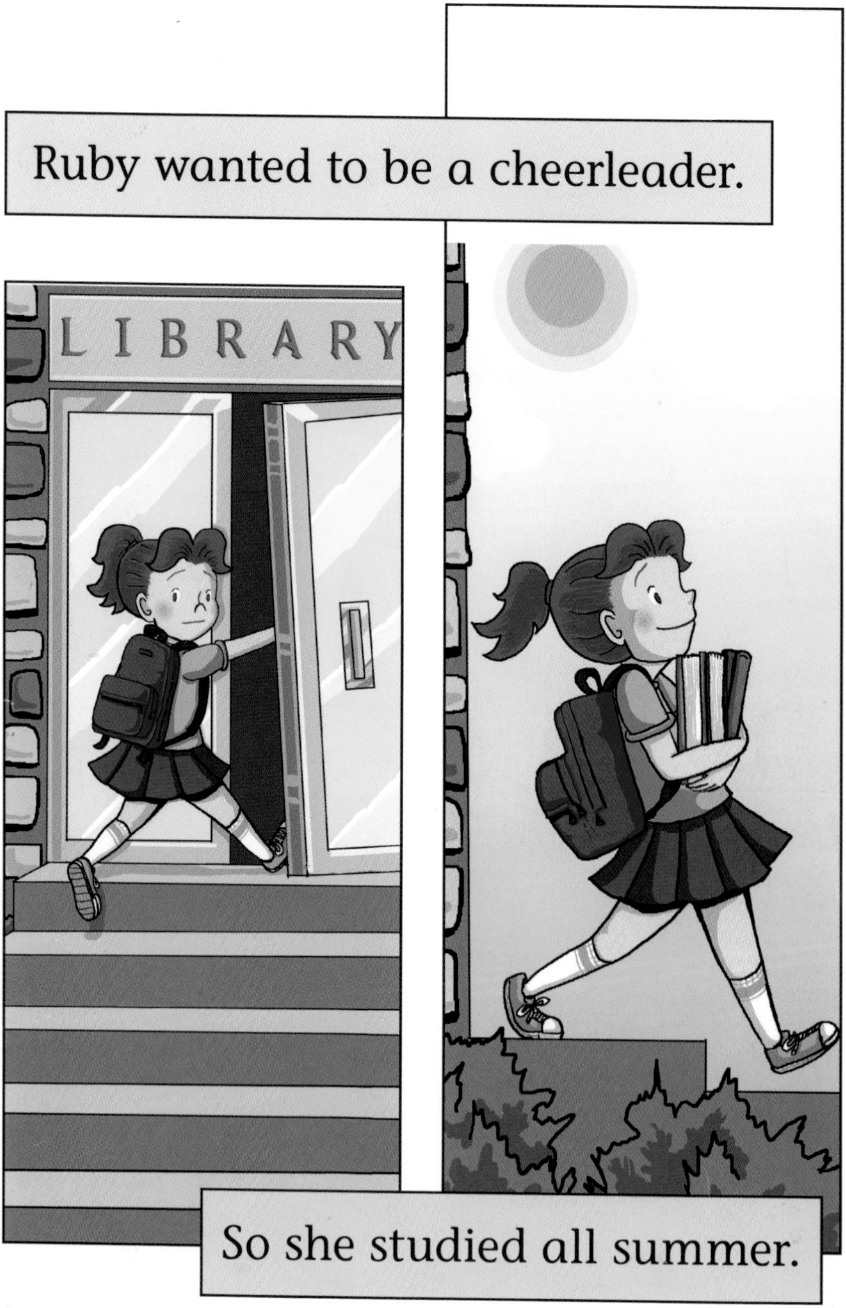
Ruby wanted to be a cheerleader.
LIBRARY
So she studied all summer.

Ruby went to the pool with her friends.

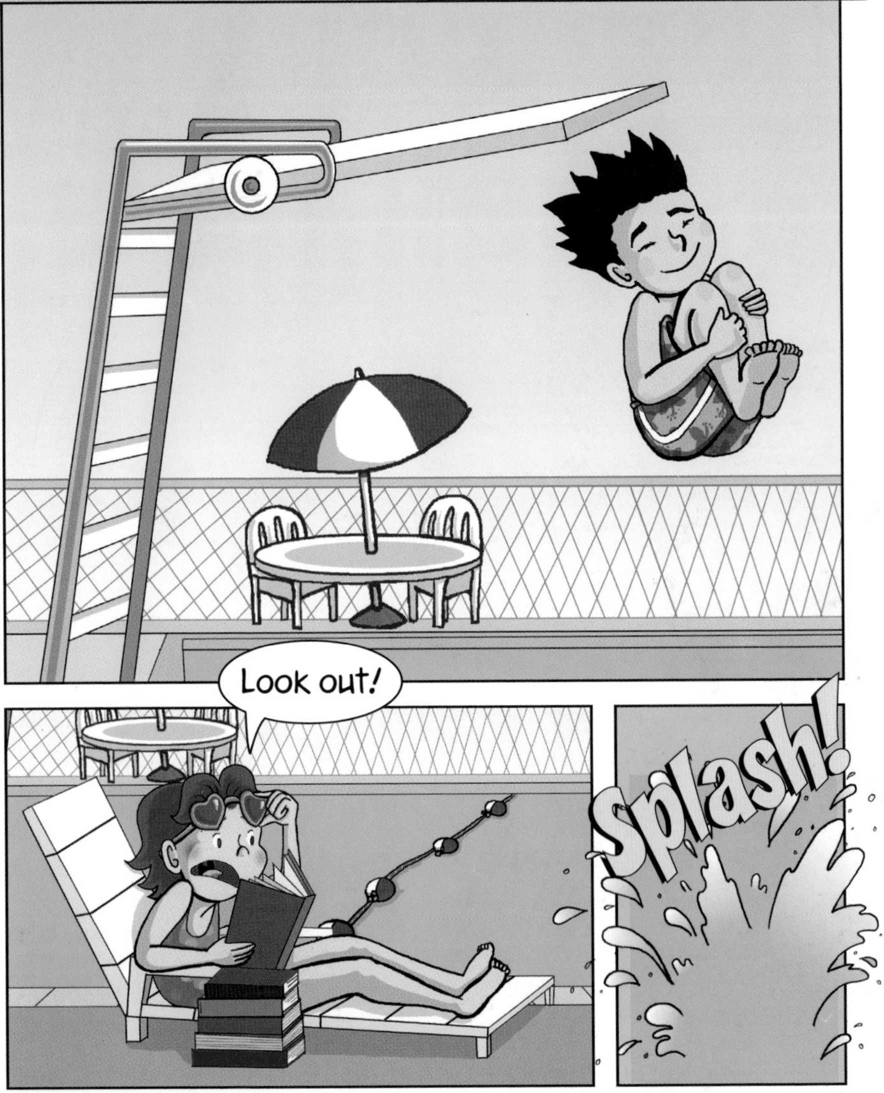
Look out!
Splash!

But Ruby did not swim. Ruby studied.

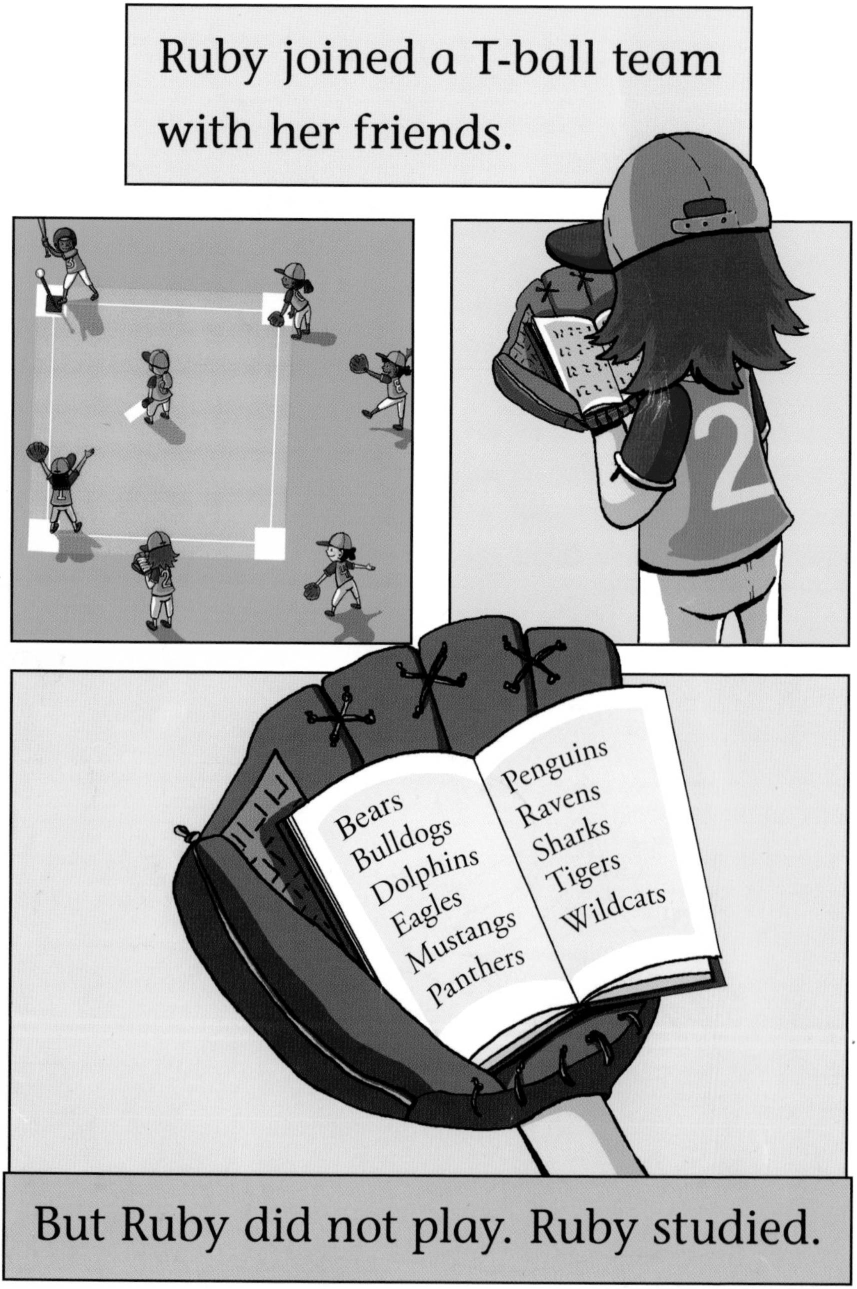
Ruby joined a T-ball team with her friends.
Bears
Bulldogs
Dolphins
Eagles
Mustangs
Panthers
Penguins
Ravens
Sharks
Tigers
Wildcats
But Ruby did not play. Ruby studied.

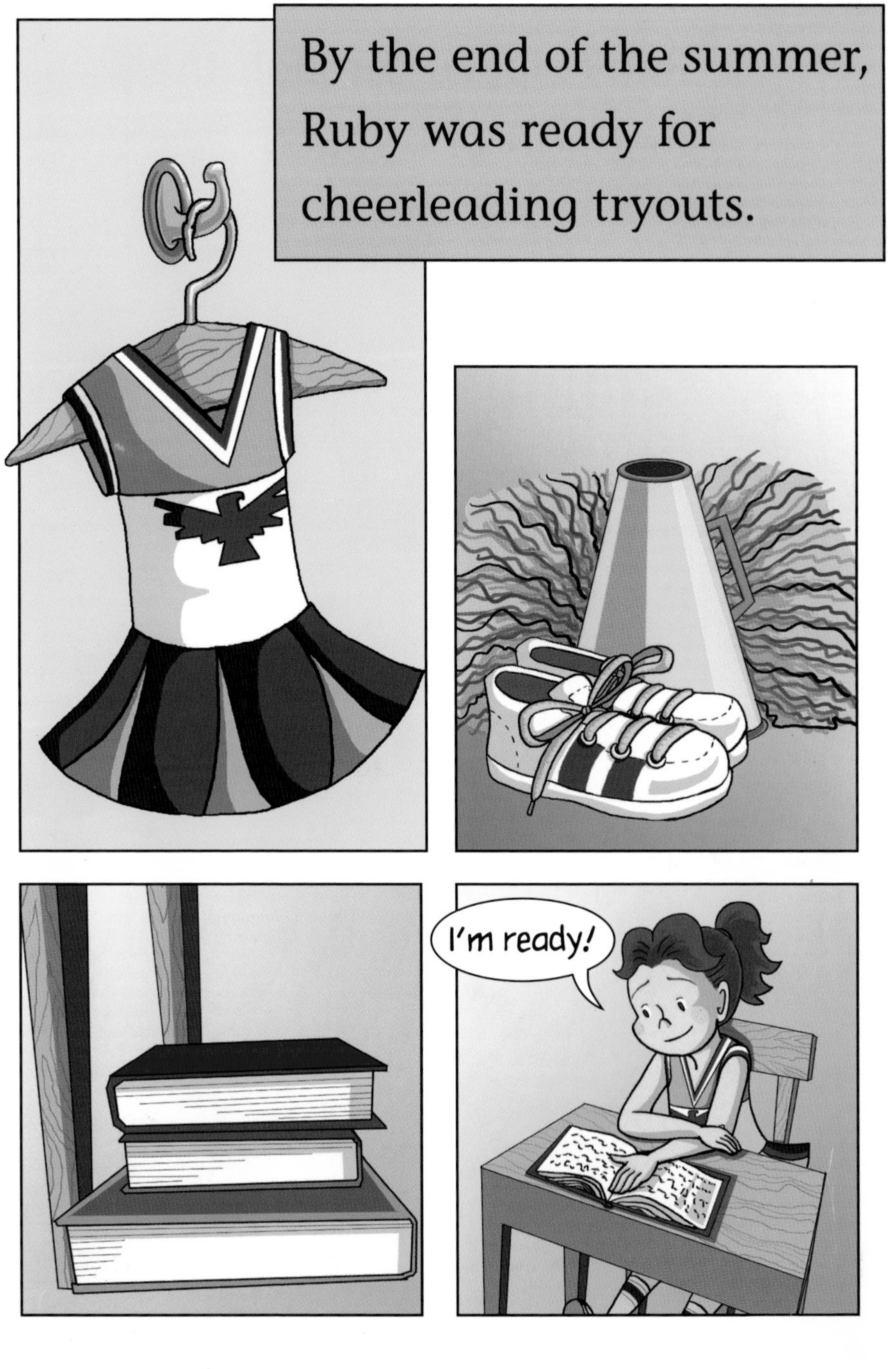
By the end of the summer, Ruby was ready for cheerleading tryouts.
I'm ready!

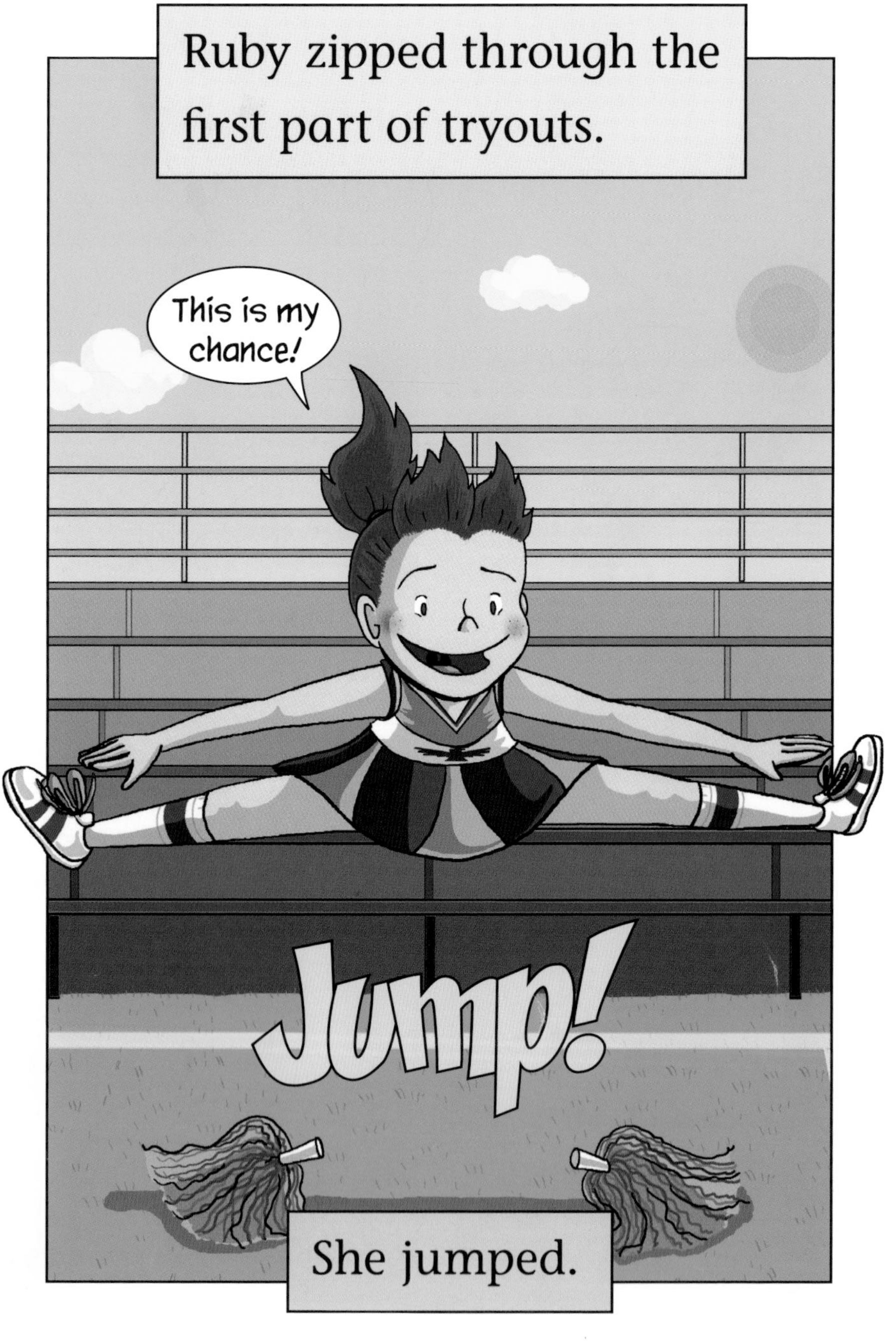
Ruby zipped through the first part of tryouts.
This is my chance!
Jump!
She jumped.

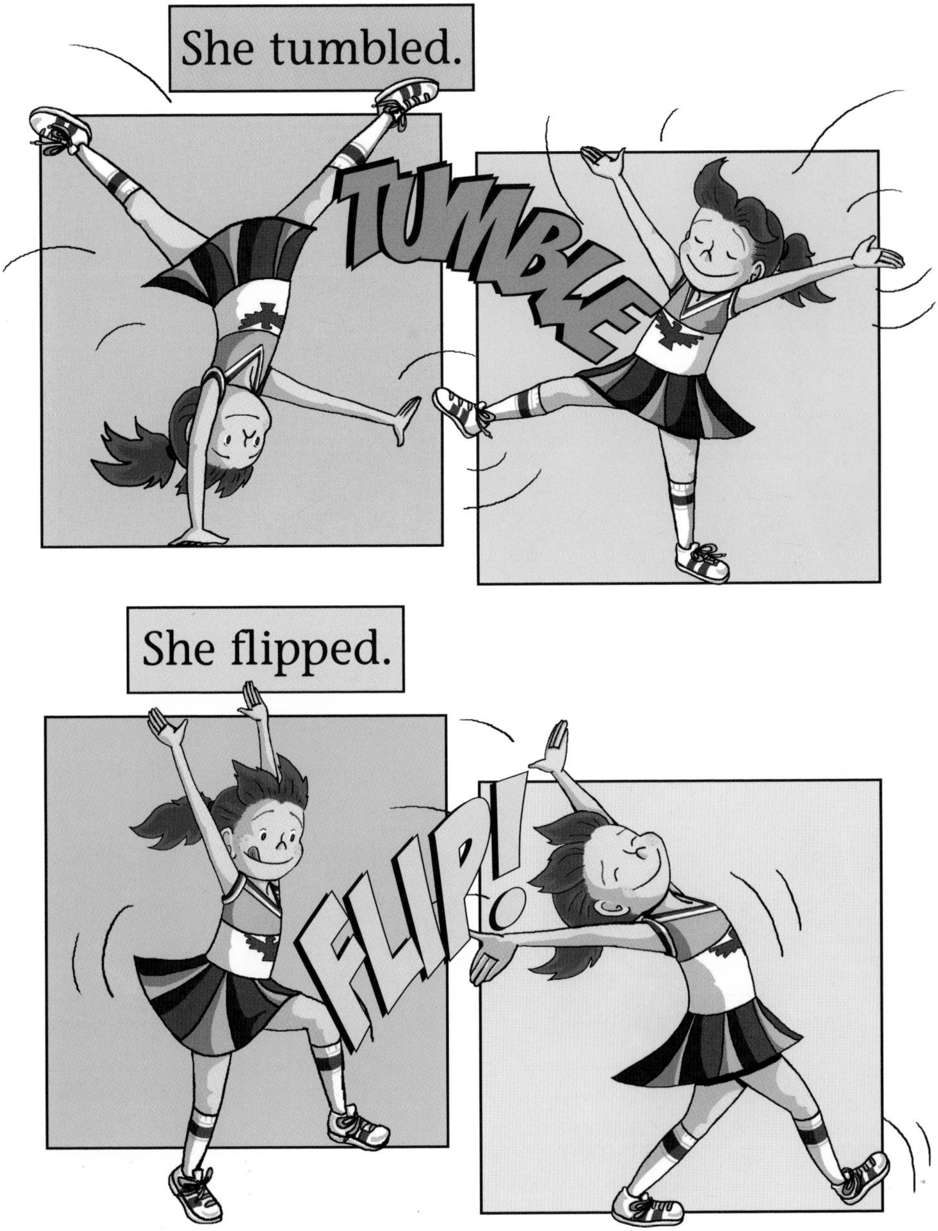
She tumbled.
TUMBLE
She flipped.
FLIP!

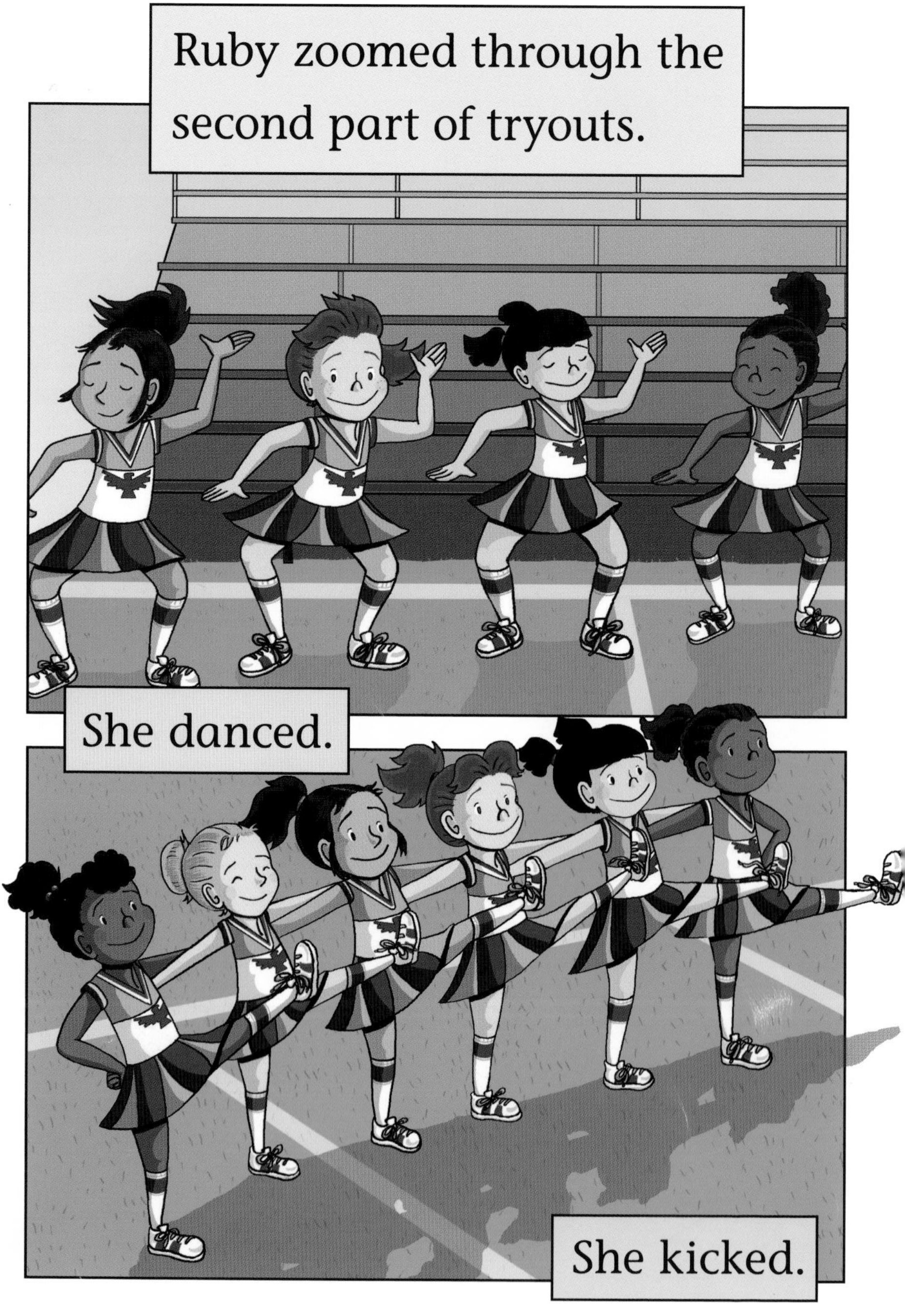
Ruby zoomed through the second part of tryouts.
She danced.
She kicked.

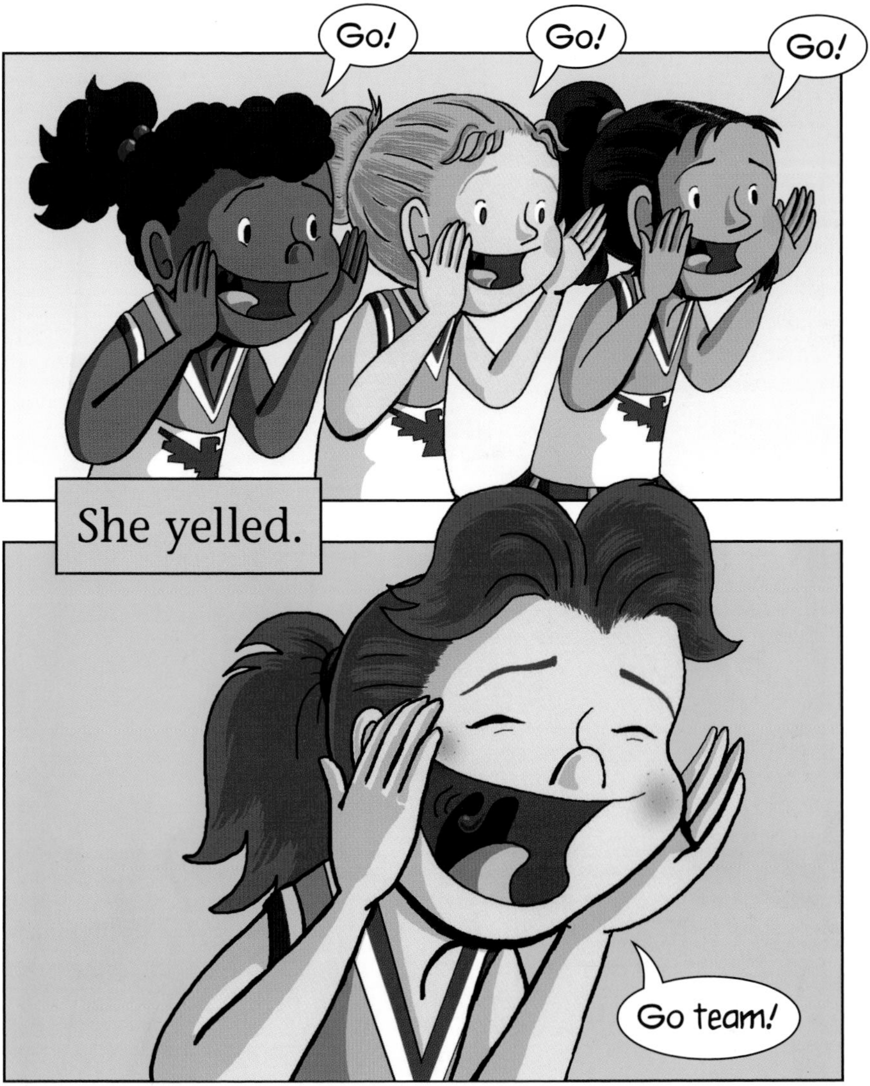
Go!
Go!
Go!
She yelled.
Go team!

Finally, it was time to cheer. Ruby had to perform two cheers. For the first one, she had to spell the team's name.

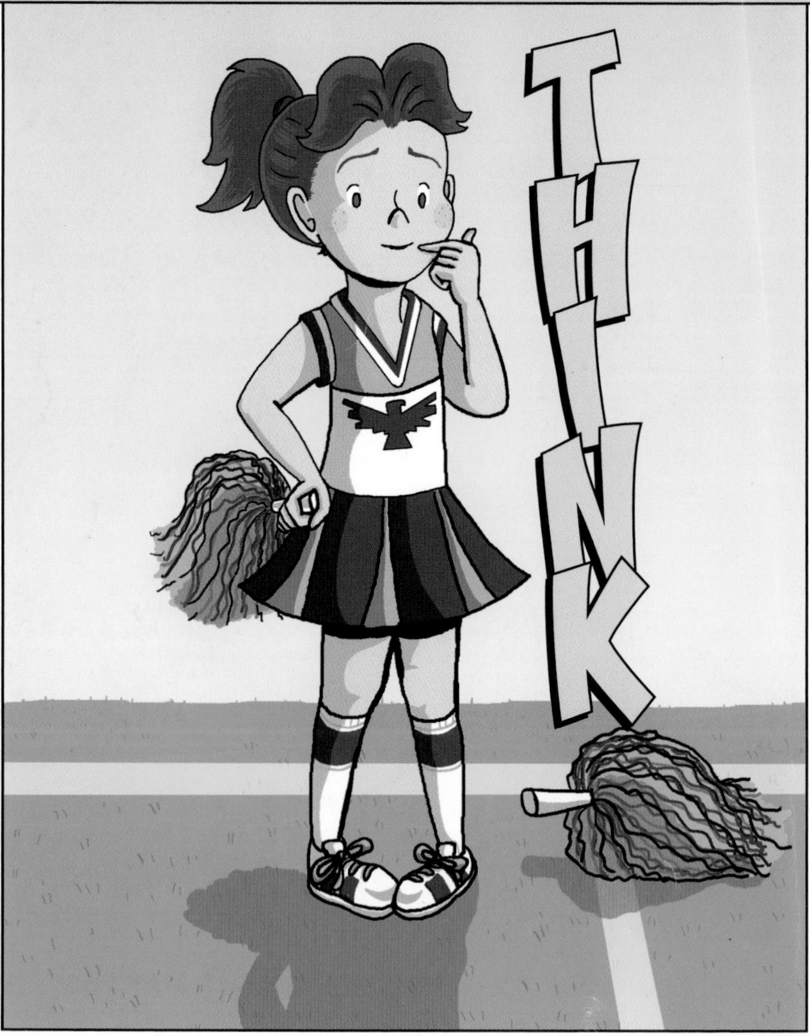
THINK

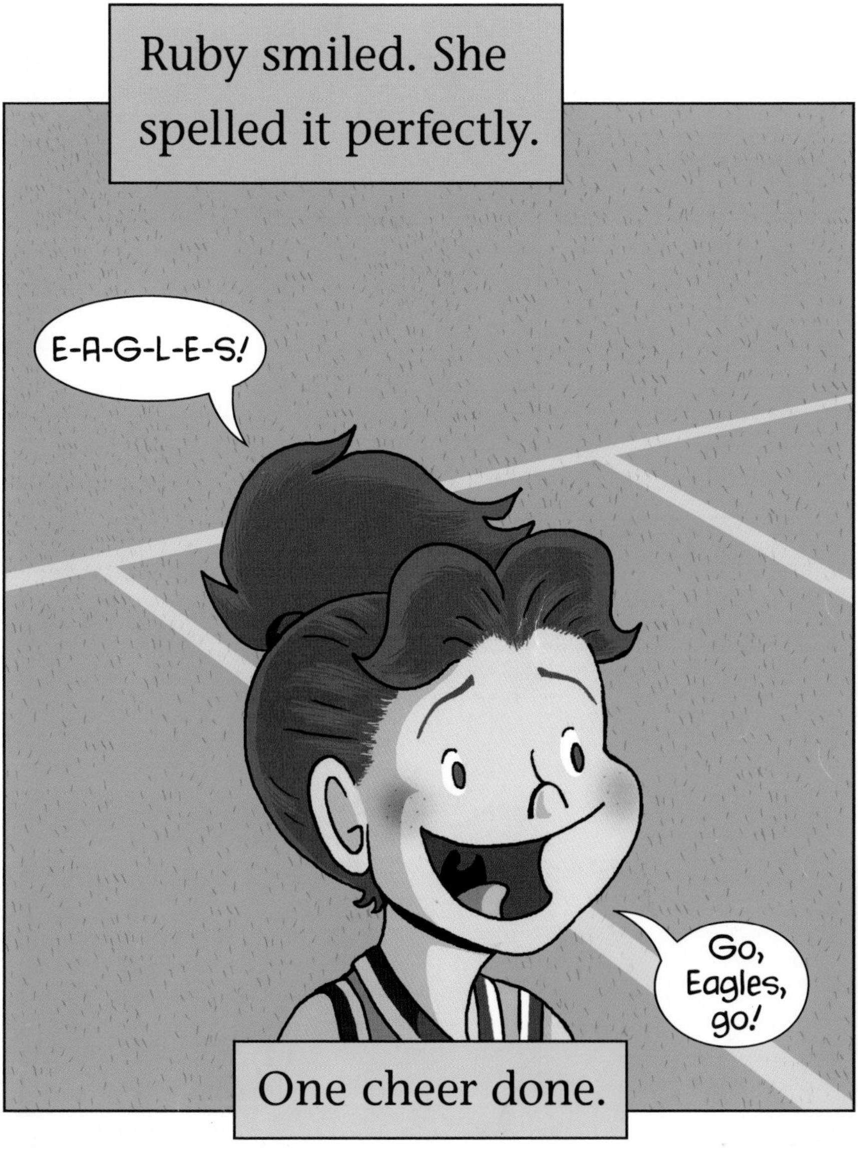
Ruby smiled. She spelled it perfectly.
E-A-G-L-E-S!
Go, Eagles, go!
One cheer done.

Next, she had to spell the word "spirit." Ruby started the cheer.

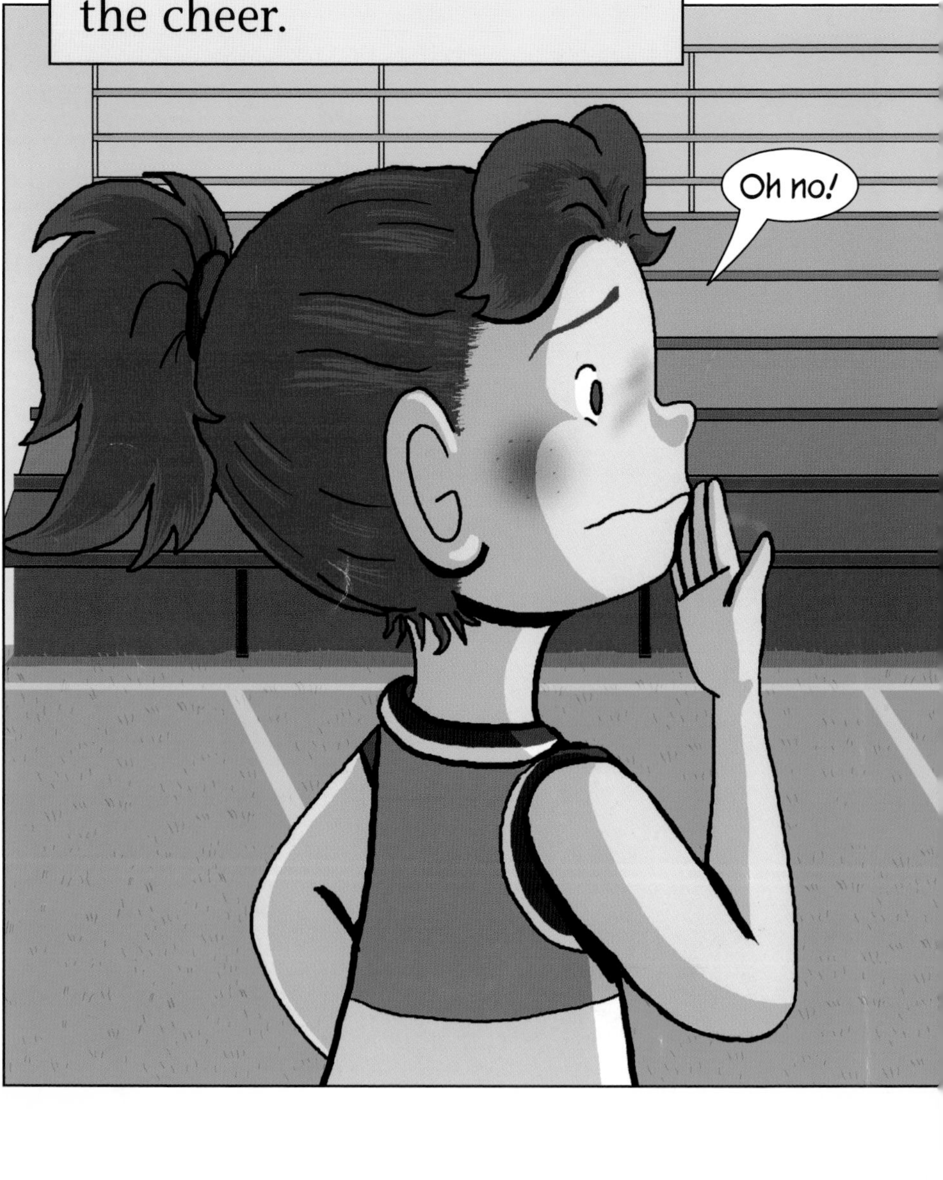
Oh no!

Then she stopped. She started again.
Then she stopped again.

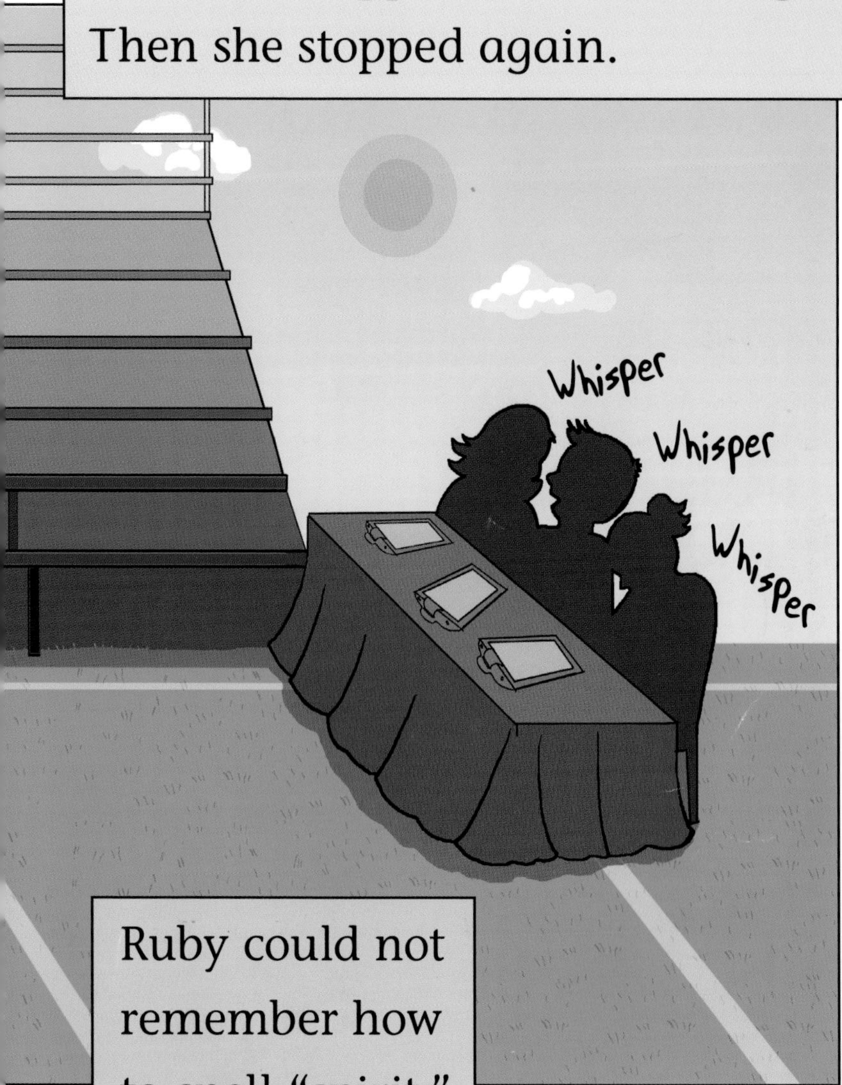
Whisper
Whisper
Whisper

Ruby could not remember how to spell "spirit."

Then Ruby thought about all of her hard work. She knew she could do it.

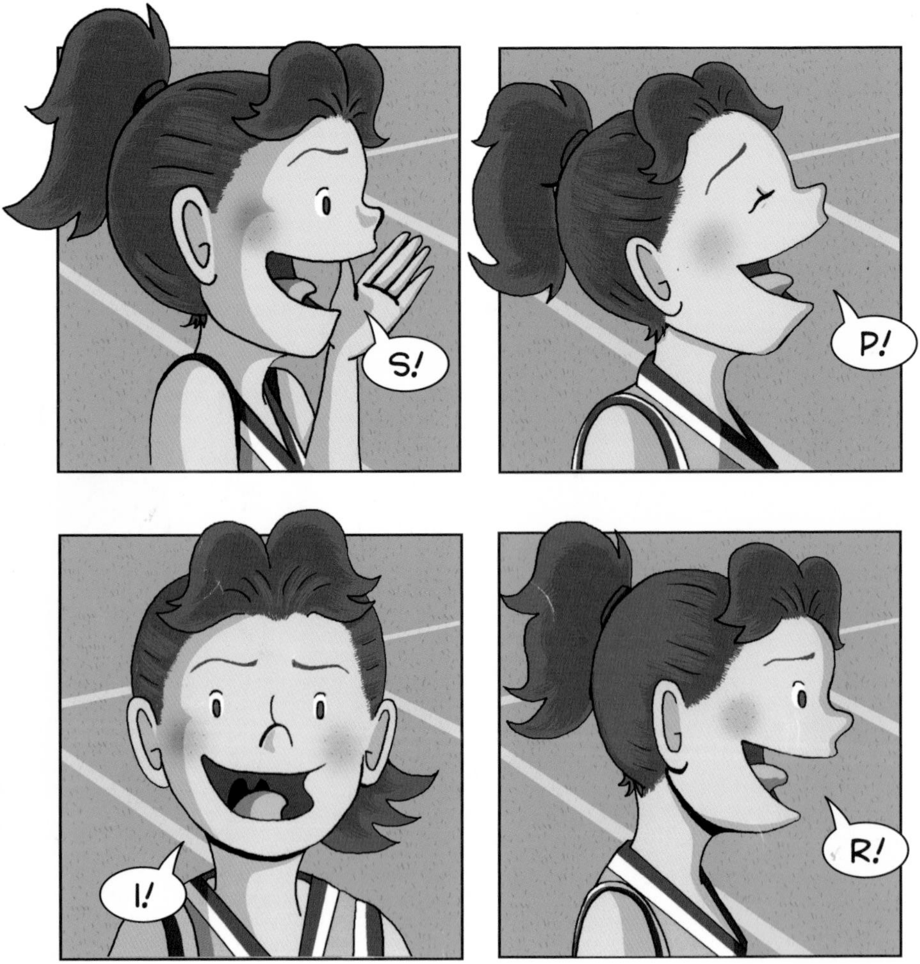
S!
P!
I!
R!

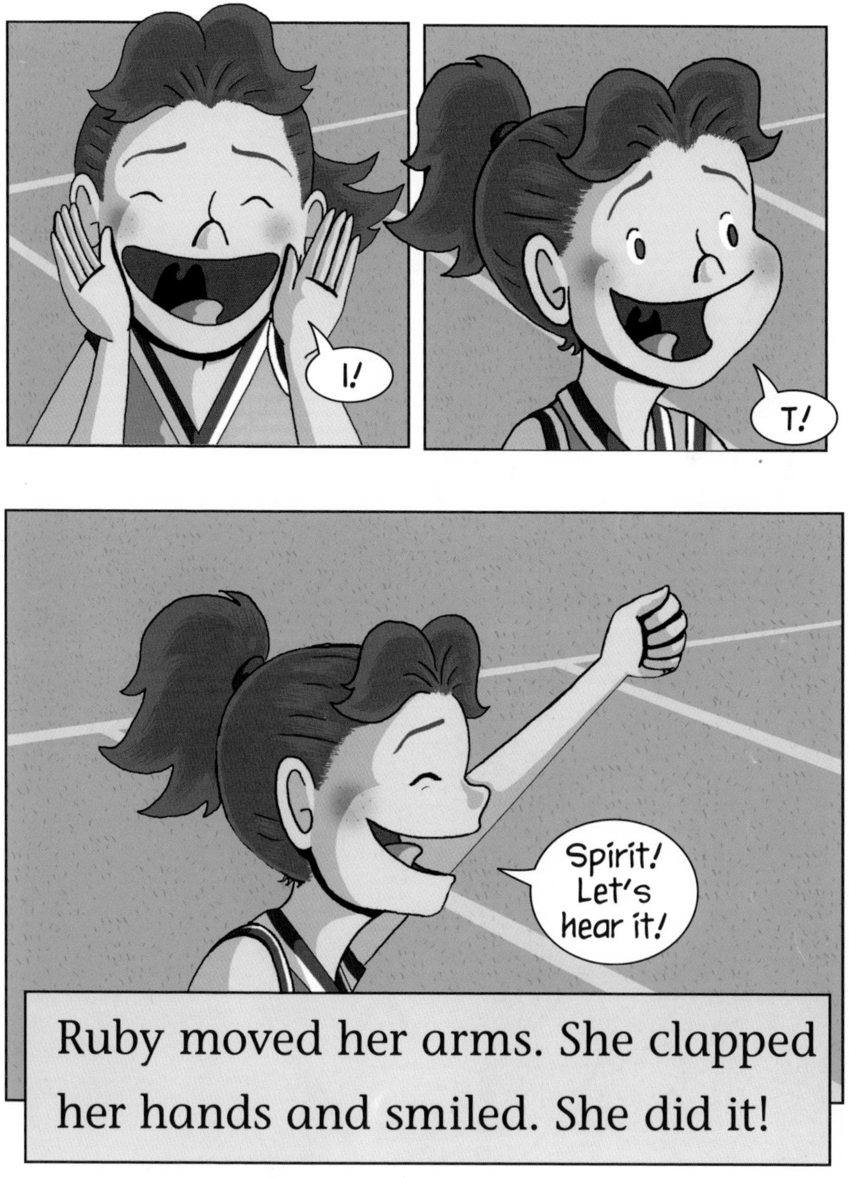
I!
T!
Spirit! Let's hear it!

Ruby moved her arms. She clapped her hands and smiled. She did it!

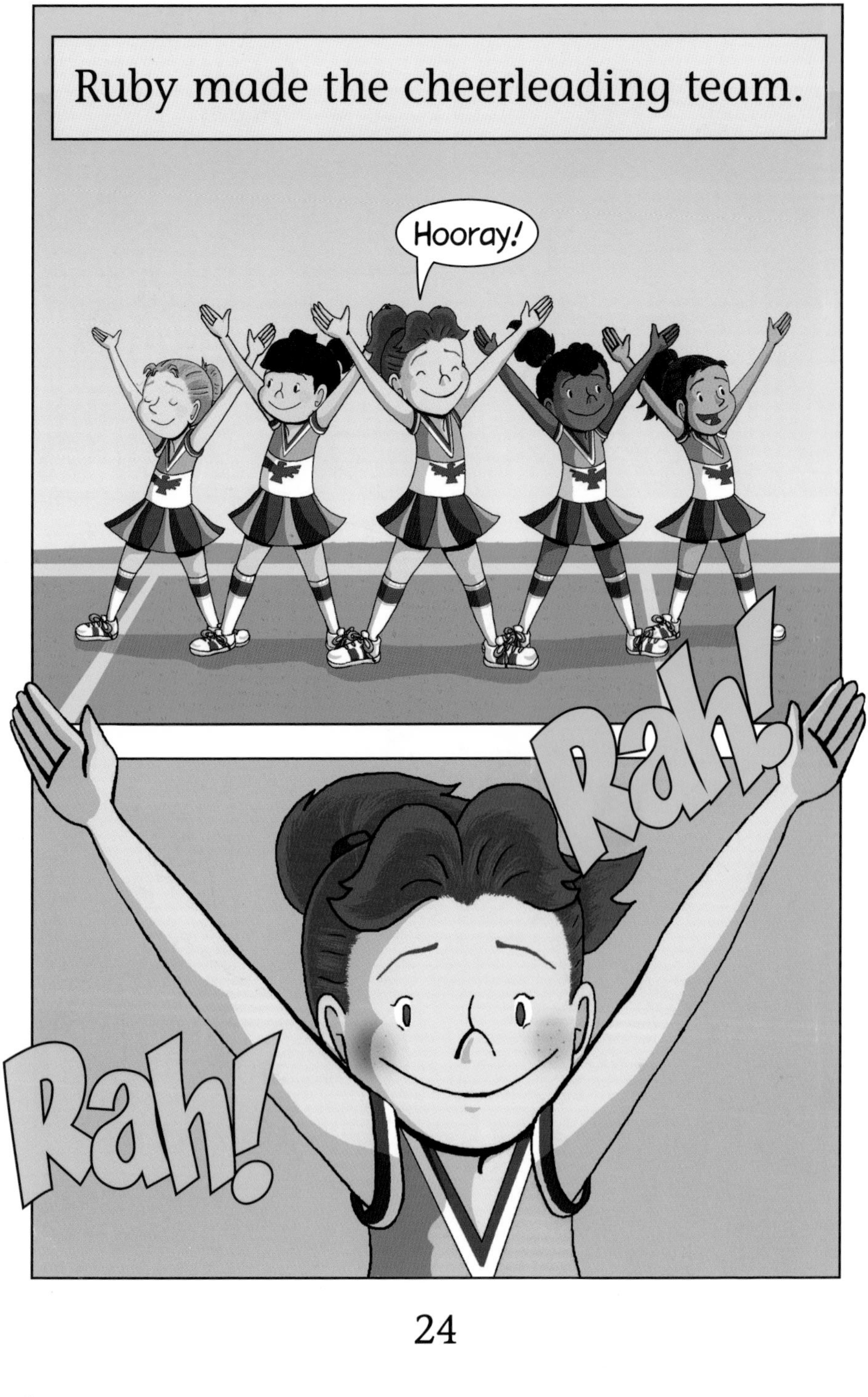
Ruby made the cheerleading team.
Hooray!
Rah!
Rah!

Ruby also won the class spelling bee. Rah-rah Ruby!

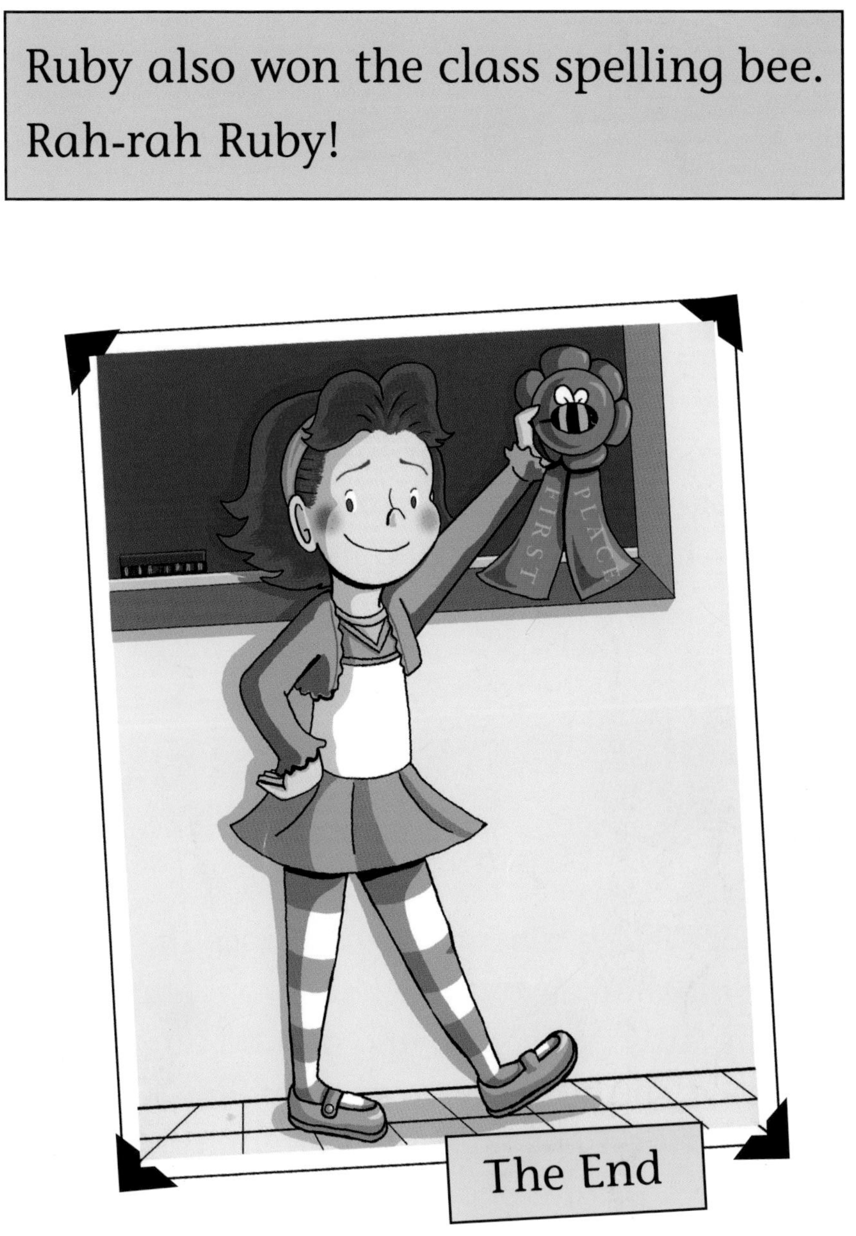
FIRST
PLACE

The End

ABOUT THE AUTHOR

Growing up in a small town with no cable (and parents who are teachers), reading was the only thing to do. Since then, Christianne Jones has read about a bazillion books and written more than 40. Christianne works as an editor and lives in Mankato, Minnesota, with her husband and daughter.

ABOUT THE ILLUSTRATOR

Cori Doerrfeld has been drawing since she was a little girl. She always knew she would grow up to be an artist. After studying art and illustration in college, she began work as a children's book illustrator. Cori has illustrated several titles, including a picture book with actress Brooke Shields. When not hard at work painting, Cori enjoys spending time with her daughter, reading comics, and spending time outdoors.

GLOSSARY

cheerleader (CHIHR-leed-ur)—a person who leads cheers at a sporting event

flip (flip)—a tumbling move where the feet go over the head

study (STUHD-ee)—to learn by reading, repeating, or looking very closely at something

tryout (TRYE-out)—a test of skills

tumble (TUHM-buhl)—a gymnastic move that includes rolling and turning

1.) Ruby had trouble spelling. Have you ever had trouble with a subject in school? If so, what was it?

2.) Ruby had to work extra hard to learn how to spell. Have you ever worked extra hard to learn something?

3.) In the end, Ruby makes the cheerleading team. She also wins the spelling bee. How else do you think learning how to spell helped Ruby?

WRITING PROMPTS

1.) Ruby does two cheers in the book. Write a cheer of your own. Then perform it for your friends and family.

2.) Ruby studied at the pool. She also studied at her T-ball game. Draw a picture of another place Ruby could have studied.

3.) Throughout the book, there are sound and action words next to some of the art. Pick at least two of those words. Then write your own sentences using those words.

THE FIRST STEP INTO GRAPHIC NOVELS

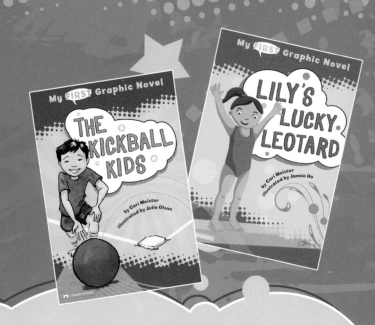

My FIRST Graphic Novel
THE KICKBALL KIDS
by Cari Meister
illustrated by Julie Olson

My FIRST Graphic Novel
LILY'S LUCKY LEOTARD
by Cari Meister
illustrated by Jannie Ho

My FIRST Graphic Novel

These books are the perfect introduction to the world of safe, appealing graphic novels. Each story uses familiar topics, repeating patterns, and core vocabulary words appropriate for a beginning reader. Combine the entertaining story with comic book panels, exciting action elements, and bright colors and a safe graphic novel is born.

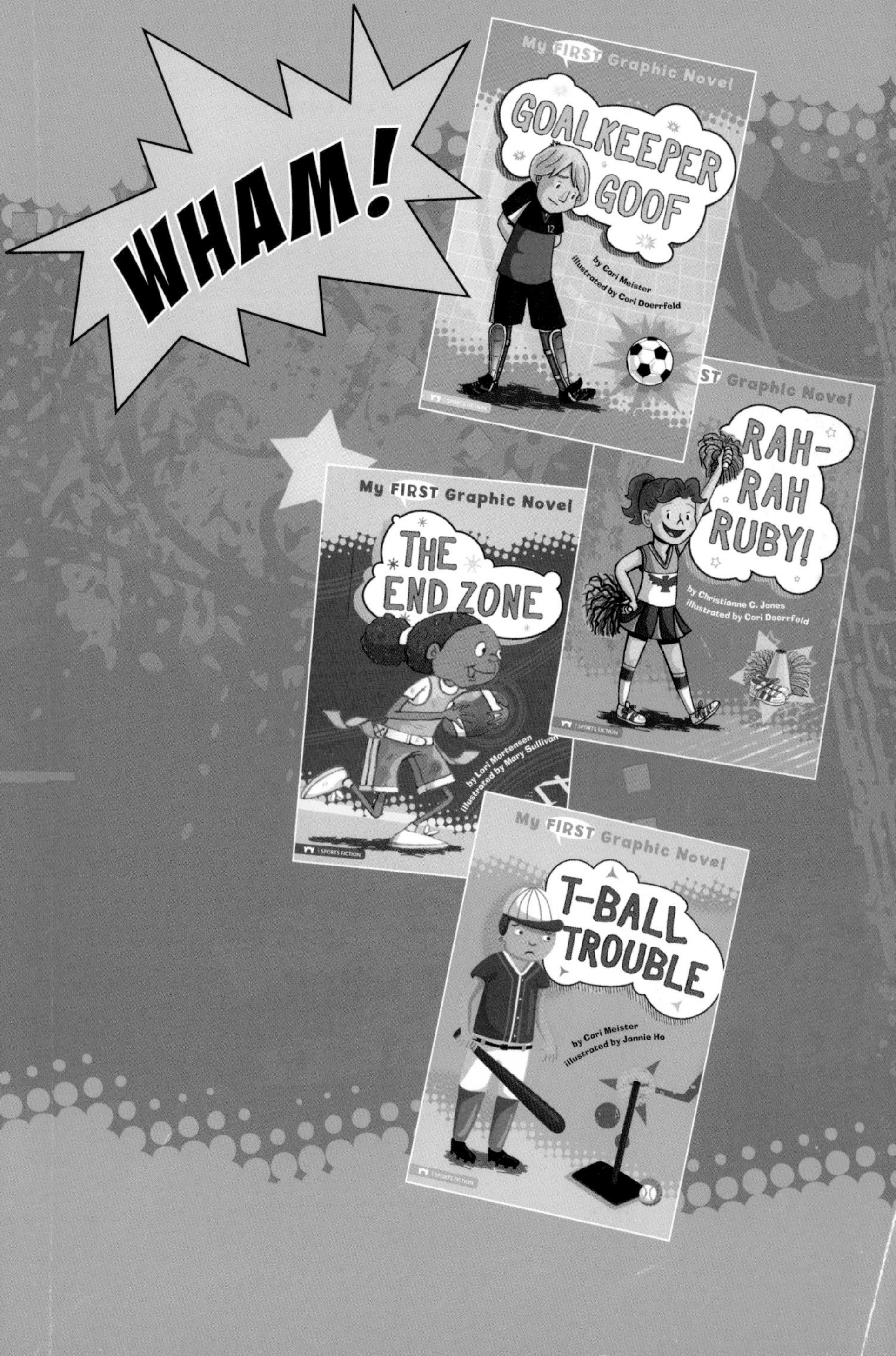

WHAM!
My FIRST Graphic Novel
GOALKEEPER GOOF
by Cari Meister
illustrated by Cori Doerrfeld
SPORTS FICTION
ST Graphic Novel
RAH-RAH RUBY!
by Christianne C. Jones
illustrated by Cori Doerrfeld
SPORTS FICTION
My FIRST Graphic Novel
THE END ZONE
by Lori Mortensen
illustrated by Mary Sullivan
SPORTS FICTION
My FIRST Graphic Novel
T-BALL TROUBLE
by Cari Meister
illustrated by Jannie Ho
SPORTS FICTION

INTERNET SITES

Do you want to know more about subjects related to this book? Or are you interested in learning about other topics? Then check out FactHound, a fun, easy way to find Internet sites.

Our investigative staff has already sniffed out great sites for you!

Here's how to use FactHound:

1. Visit *www.facthound.com*

2. Select your grade level.

3. To learn more about subjects related to this book, type in the book's ISBN number: 143421298.

4. Click the Fetch It button.

FactHound will fetch the best Internet sites for you!